WHO'S IN THE SHED?

by Brenda Parkes
illustrated by Ester Kasepuu

Down at the farm
one Saturday night,
the animals woke
with a **terrible** fright.

There was *howling*
and *growling*
and *roaring*
and *clawing*

as something was led
from a truck
to the shed.

"Who's in the shed?"
everyone said.
"Who's in the shed?"

"Let me have a peep,"
baaed the big white sheep.
"Let me have a peep."

So the sheep had a peep
through a hole in the shed.
What did she see?

"My turn now,"
mooed the sleek brown cow.
"My turn now."

So the cow had a peep
through a hole in the shed.
What did she see?

"Let me see in there," neighed the old gray mare. **"Let me see in there."**

So the mare had a peep
through a hole in the shed.
What did she see?

"What is it then?"
clucked the little red hen.
"What is it then?"

So the hen had a peep
through a hole in the shed.
What did she see?

"It's something big,"
grunted the fat pink pig.
"It's something big."

So the pig had a peep
through a hole in the shed.
What did she see?

roared the circus bear.

And everyone ran

away

from

there.